Ghost Hexed

Valley Ghosts Series Book Four

BL Maxwell

BL Maxwell

Valley Ghosts Series Book Four

BL Maxwell

Copyright

Warning

Intended for a mature an 18+ audience only. This book contains material that may be offensive to some and is intended for a mature, adult audience. It contains graphic language, explicit sexual content, and adult situations.

Dedication

Happy Halloween, to everyone who loves Jimbo.

Chapter One

First Official Date

Jimbo

"So, you want to go or not?" I barked at Dean. He ignored me as usual, and without missing a beat, continued with his inventory as if I hadn't said a word. "Dean?" I tried again, not so snappy this time.

"What is it, James? I'm sorry, I didn't hear you?" he said as he looked up at me with a sexy grin and the greenest eyes I'd ever seen. His dark brown hair was shorter and neater than it had been when I'd first laid eyes on him, but the years gave him an edgier look that was both hot and classy. What the hell did he see in me? I had no clue, but I was thankful for whatever the fuck it was. "You're staring again," he said, with an eye roll and a shake of his head.

"Sorry, still don't know what it is you see in me, but I'm glad for whatever it is." He stood from where he sat at one of the dining room tables and moved over to where I sat across from him. With no warning he straddled me and smoothed one of his hands over my head that really was due for a shaving and cupped my chin with the other.

"You were the hottest chef at culinary school, and now you're my hot boyfriend." He leaned in and brushed his lips lightly over mine before gripping my face with both hands and having his way with my mouth.

"Dammit, Dean," I panted out; this man got to me more than anyone ever had, before or after him. He drew his tongue across my lips and leaned just out of my reach when I tried to kiss him again. He leaned in close enough I could feel his smile ghost across my mouth, and when he thrust his groin against mine, I clenched my teeth so I didn't blow right there.

"Was there something you wanted to ask me?" he whispered.

"Fuck, what you do to me—it should be illegal, but I'm so damn glad it's not."

He huffed out a laugh, and when he tried to stand up from my lap, I gripped his thighs and kept him there. "Where do you think you're going? I have something I wanted to ask you, but you used your power of sexual persuasion on me, and you know I can't resist you."

He pulled back and looked me in the eye. "You resisted me for twenty years," he accused, with an arch of his brow.

"I tried to keep you safe. To keep us both safe. I didn't want to expose you to any paranormal dangers that go with dating someone like me," I explained, knowing he knew all this, but it didn't make me feel any less guilty for freezing him out all those years ago.

His face softened, and he leaned his forehead against mine. "I know, I'm just messing with you. And I can't be too mad at the ghosts, since that's what brought you back to me. Well, not too mad, or terrified. Mostly terrified."

I hugged him close to me and breathed into his neck. "I want to take you to something fun, can we go do something fun together? No ghosts, no Jason or Wade. Just you and me," I asked without meeting his eyes.

His finger on my chin forced me to look directly at him. "I would love to go spend the day with you doing something that doesn't include work or ghosts. What did you have in mind?"

"I thought we could go out to Gibson Ranch and watch the Civil War reenactment. I went years ago, and it was cool, I mean if you're into all that history stuff."

"I'm into all that James stuff. I love finding out more about you, and if this is something that appeals to you, then I'm up for checking it out."

"Yeah?" I asked, not sure he was serious. His eyes were locked on mine, and I couldn't look away. Didn't want to. For once in my life I was right where I wanted to be. He leaned forward and kissed my lips so sweetly it made my damn heart hurt. He was everything.

"Yes, I'd love to spend a beautiful fall day watching grown men run around, acting out a battle that didn't even take place in California," he said, voice flat, and giving away no clues to how he really felt.

My eyes bounced back and forth between his as I searched for something that would tell me if he was joking or serious. Fuck, I sucked at this. "James, yes, I want to go," he finally said with a laugh.

I slumped forward and rested my forehead against his shoulder. "Fuck, you know I have no clue when you're joking, right?" I responded, sounding a little too desperate, which made me cringe.

"Aw, you know I love how honest and quirky you are. Come on, let's plan this ghost-free excursion." He stood up from me and held his hand out. The sound of my phone broke the spell he once again had me under, and he leaned in and kissed me before walking back to the office. I dug my phone out of my pocket and looked at the screen.

"What the fuck do you want, Wade?"

"Well, hello to you too, asshole," he snapped back in reply.

I took a deep breath and dragged my hand over my face before I said another word. "Sorry, Wade, you caught me off guard. What did you want?"

"Hey, Jimbo, just sounds like you're being your usual charming self to me. Nothing new there," he said with a laugh. I smiled, partly in relief he wasn't pissed, that he gave me shit and let it go. "I was just calling to check in, we have that new job out in Ione, and I wanted to go on a tour. You feel like tagging along?"

"When are you going?" It intrigued me, I'd never been to Preston Castle, and after they had invited us to investigate it, I'd found a lot of information online.

"We'll probably go before Halloween and check out the haunted house attraction."

"No, we won't," I heard in the background. "Is that Jason?"

"Yeah, he's still a little touchy after what happened at The Hitching Post," Wade said.

"No I'm not," I heard again through the phone.

"What the fuck!? Is he still afraid of the fake haunted houses?" I asked, remembering how he was last year when we all went. I heard a sigh, and the sound of a door sliding shut.

"He's still afraid of the fake haunted houses," Wade said.

"Oh damn, I was hoping to take Dean with us."

"We'll go, don't worry. Jason won't want to miss it, but he'll be miserable the whole time. Which means he'll need me to protect him," he said with a chuckle, before I heard what had to be a slap.

"Hey, dammit, Jason," Wade said, and I heard them scuffling and laughing. I hated to admit how damn cute they were.

"Hey, Jimbo," Jason said. "I looked online, and there are tours we can go on that aren't during the haunted house they have going on there at Halloween."

"Whatever, just admit you don't want to go to the haunted house."

"Fuck you, Jimbo," Jason said, and I heard another scuffle.

"Figure out a date and we'll be there," I said, and hung up.

"So, James," Dean said, walking toward me. "When are we going to this reenactment?"

Chapter Two

Fall Leaves

Dean

It was a perfect fall day when we drove toward the park where the reenactment would be held. "This is beautiful here, I've never been to this area," I said as I reached across the center console to squeeze James's hand.

"You've never been to Gibson Ranch? We used to go on field trips here when I was a kid," James said.

"Nope, I didn't grow up around here, didn't move to the Sacramento area until I was out of high school."

"I forgot about that, so I'm taking you somewhere you've never been on our first real date."

"This is a date? You never said it was a date," I teased, knowing James couldn't take being teased.

"Fuck yes it's a date, I asked you, you said yes, we're going somewhere together. It's a date," he insisted, as I looked out the side window to hide my amusement. He was so easy to get to. Which was probably why Wade and Jason gave him such a hard time. Finally, I couldn't hold back any longer and a laugh burst out of me. "What the fuck, Dean? Are you laughing at me?" He tried to pull his hand away, look convincingly pissed, and drive, all at the same time.

"It's a date, the best date ever. I really am excited to see what this is all about. I've never been to a reenactment, and it really is beautiful out here." I patted his hand as I spoke, hoping it helped to calm him down a little. "Sorry, James," I whispered, and raised his hand up to my lips. "Can you ever forgive me?" He glanced over at me with a look on his face that said what the fuck, and I watched as his face softened and he glanced at me with a look that made my heart clench. That was what I truly loved about James, he was gruff and grouchy on the outside, but he had a heart of gold. And that heart was all mine. "I love you," I said under my breath.

"What was that?" he asked, and leaned on the center console to get closer to me. We'd both said those words the night we were trapped in the basement, but I was waiting for a special place to tell him again. Sometime when neither of us were in fear for our lives.

"Nothing, just looking at the fall colors."

"Fall colors?" He shook his head and turned to look out the side window, but his dimple gave him away, and I had to make myself stay in my seat rather than crawling over the console to get closer to him.

"Fall colors. I really am excited about this, James, thanks for asking me to go." He nodded and wove our fingers together. We drove past a road I recognized. "Dyer Lane, why is that familiar to me?" I mumbled, thinking out loud.

"You probably saw a story about it on the news, it has quite a history. I'll tell you all about it sometime, it's been on the local television stations, usually around Halloween. Which is why you won't catch me driving in this area by myself after dark. Not that I'm over in this area much, I'm mostly over at Wade and Jason's."

"And Wade's mom's place." I huffed, not even trying to hide it.

"You know she guilts me into it, that woman has some weird power of persuasion," James explained.

"Aw, you're just a big softie," I said, making him scowl.

"You haven't tried to tell her no yet. You wait, there will come a time when she'll ask you something you don't want to answer, and somehow you'll be telling her exactly what she wants to know without realizing why you're doing it." His voice took on an edge of panic at the thought of it.

"I'll take your word for it. Maybe we could invite her and her husband to join us at the restaurant. Make a night of it?"

"Oh god, Dean, you really want to put us at her mercy? If we have dinner with them, she'll know everything about us. And I do mean *everything*." He punctuated it with a shiver.

"O-kay, maybe we can stop by her house and just stay hello sometime," I said. "I just want to get to know your friends better. You're all so close, and I want to be part of that with you, be a part of your life." I hoped I didn't sound pathetic, but I wanted to be honest with him. I wouldn't sit back and be quiet this time and let him decide for me. He'd chosen not to pursue a relationship with me years ago, hoping to protect me from the spirits he had no control over. But now he was stronger, he understood his power more. And so did I. Or I hoped I did. It wasn't like I could go take a class on "how to understand your boyfriend's power to pull spirits to him." I knew his friends would keep him safe, or they'd try like hell, anyway. And I'd be there too, doing anything I could to help.

"So, tell me more about Dyer Lane, it's such a weird name for a street," I said, bringing the conversation back to it. "What was it you said about it being on the news?"

"It's haunted," James said.

"Right, how can a road be haunted?"

"Look it up, there's been a lot of different things reported there for years. It all started in the 1930s when some girls were attacked and killed. They were rumored to have been witches. They cursed the guys that attacked them, and all of them died soon after in very mysterious ways," James said. "Then there's the ghost of a farmer driving his tractor, a ghost of a policeman in his patrol car, a satanic cult, and even the KKK. Apparently Dyer Lane was a crazy place over the years."

"How do you know all this?" I asked, and he heaved out a big sigh before he answered.

"Fucking Jason, he knows every haunted place around here, and has either dragged Wade to them, or wants to go there. They checked this place out years ago but didn't have any experiences, much to Wade's extreme relief."

"Poor Wade, the things you do for love, right?" I said with a smile.

"They've both gone above and beyond, if Jason hadn't been at the restaurant with Wade . . . I'm not sure what would have happened. To any of us. That was crazy as hell."

Just thinking about it made me tense, and he noticed. "Hey, it's okay. That wasn't a normal case, we had no way of knowing there was one entity that was hell-bent on possessing Wade."

"I hope you're right, and I hope none of you are ever in danger like that again. Seeing you thrown across the room terrified me. I had no idea a ghost could do that. I mean I've seen it in movies, but I never in a million years thought it could be true." My mind went back to that moment, when I expected to find James seriously hurt. He was hurled so forcefully at the wall, I imagined the worst. To say I was relieved to find him unconscious but still alive was an understatement. "Maybe put some distance between us and Dyer Lane?" I felt him speed up and relaxed a little more.

The road ahead narrowed, and it seemed we went from city to country in a matter of a mile. The trees were thicker here, and their colors painted the sides of the road in a wall of yellows and reds. The smell of leaves and fresh country air permeated the area. Both of us were silent as we enjoyed the beauty all around us.

"This is it," James said as he signaled a right turn into what looked like a big open dirt parking lot. We followed the line of cars in front of us until we could finally find a parking space. Stepping out of the car, James walked over to me, taking my hand and tugging me toward the area that appeared to be a park. Complete with rolling hills, green grass, ancient oak trees, and a large pond, it really was stunning. As we walked closer, there were tents arranged in different areas around the park, men dressed in the blue of the Northern Union armies, and others in the gray of the Southern Confederates.

"James, this is amazing, almost like stepping back in time," I said, unable to hold back a smile. Some ladies dressed in the long dresses of that era fanned themselves as they walked by with a nod of hello to us. It truly felt like we had traveled back in time and were dropped into an alternative universe where the Civil War had been fought here in California. A group of men on horseback raced across a grassy knoll, a flag streaming behind them.

"Come on, let's go see what they're up to," I said as we moved to follow them. When we reached where they now were all dismounted, there were white canvas tents set up as a camp, a small fire pit for cooking, and strung between some tents was a laundry line. We walked around and took it all in. Everyone was so full of information and seemed to know everything about what it was like to live at that time in history.

We ended up at an area set up as a trading post, and wandered around looking at all the canteens, hats, and other wares they had for sale. Finally we lined up with everyone else to watch the battle reenactment. "This is incredible, I never thought I'd see something like this here," I said, completely in awe of the sight before me. Horses lined both sides of the field, and hundreds of men and boys in uniform stood with their guns at the ready. The cannons fired, startling us all, and the men slowly marched toward each other, kneeling to shoot a single shot before standing and reloading their guns. They continued this way, many of them falling in mock deaths until the survivors met at the center and continued their fight in hand-to-hand combat, rushing at one another with the bayonets on their guns held at the ready. It was easy to imagine it all was real, and I was thankful it wasn't.

They continued to battle until most were either taken prisoner or were lying where they had fallen in mock-death. The cannons fired a time or two more, making everyone wince and cover their ears. It was all quite exciting, and really was fun, in a weird way. Mostly it made me glad to have not actually lived through something like this. At the end, the commanding officers had a small ceremony where one surrendered to the other, then everyone jumped up off the ground where they'd been lying and milled around with the spectators, who clapped and cheered at their performance.

"Want to walk around a while longer? We can check out all the different trades they have set up all over the place," James said. "I'm curious about the blacksmith's shop, and the chuck wagon." He smiled and tugged me along toward the various areas that were designated by their different jobs.

"Of course you want to see the chuck wagon, and just so we're clear, we are not going into the chuck wagon business. Wait, is there a chuck wagon business?" I asked, as he hurried us along.

"I have no clue, but we're about to find out." We walked up to where a wagon was set up, the side open with pots and crockery lined up on a wooden shelf. A fire blazed nearby with a large Dutch oven suspended by a tripod. James walked up to an older man with a graying beard, round glasses, and wearing suspenders. "Pardon me, can you tell me how they would have cooked while they were traveling in a covered wagon?" James asked. The man smiled, and before I knew it, they were discussing the intricacies of cooking for a group over an open fire, and I realized how happy it made me that James was enjoying himself. He might be a grouch, but he was my grouch.

Chapter Three

Car Problems

Jimbo

"That was so amazing!" I shouted in excitement as we walked away from Dave, the chuck wagon guy. He had so much information, and I wanted to try it all so bad, I could barely contain my excitement. "Maybe we could have a BBQ day at the restaurant. We could use that little park at the end of the street by the museum, or maybe—"

"James, I love that you're so enthusiastic over this, but maybe we can try it at home first and see how it goes before we throw it out there for our customers," Dean said, once again the voice of reason, and I needed a voice of reason.

"Yeah, we could do that, maybe invite Jason and Wade over. God, and Deidra too, she'd never forgive me. I need to go buy a Dutch oven first and build a fire pit. We should probably do it at my house, it's woodsier there," I said with a nod. The more I talked about it, the more I liked that idea. The guys had been to my restaurant, but not my house. Hell, Dean hadn't been to either. Most of what we did was around the Sacramento area, so in the short time we'd been together, I'd slowly moved my things to his place.

"James, I love that idea. Maybe we could do sort of a fall celebration, it's all the rage right now. I love the thought of inviting everyone to your place. Maybe then I'll finally get to see where you live, and you can show me your restaurant." He punctuated his statement with a raised brow, that I found so damn sexy, it distracted me for a moment. I shook my head to bring me back to our conversation.

"I love it, we can invite whoever you want—hell, we can even invite some of the locals in Coloma. Make a real celebration of it. What do you say, Dean?"

"I say hell yes." I couldn't hold back the laugh that burst out of me, and I pulled him close and kissed the top of his head.

"Come on, let's get going, everyone's nearly gone. We're the late stragglers we hate when we're trying to close up." We walked hand in hand through the different areas where the cavalry horses were being loaded into trailers, the tents were being taken down, and fires were being extinguished.

"We really are the last ones here, I didn't even notice. Thanks for bringing me here, James, I had a wonderful time, and it was a great first date." The feeling his words gave me was something I felt like I'd been searching a lifetime for. For the first time in my life, I lived to make him happy. I'd do whatever it took to see a smile on his face and hear his wonderful, contagious laugh. I looked at him and smiled, something I found myself doing way more in his presence.

"Yeah, time flies, I guess. I had a great time too, Dean. Thanks for indulging me, I know you weren't sure about coming here, but I'm glad you enjoyed it."

"Of course I enjoyed it, I enjoy everything I do with you, silly man."

I pulled him even closer into my side, and once again was thankful to whatever deity had seen fit to put us in each other's path again.

The sun was just setting as we walked to the car, the fall breeze turning a little chilly. I unlocked the doors, and we both climbed in, glad to be out of the cold. I turned to face Dean and took both his hands in mine, rubbing them to warm them. "Want to get some dinner on the way home? I could go for a greasy burger."

"That sounds great," he said with a shiver. I pressed the button to start my car and . . . nothing. Not even a click. Dean peered over at me with a look of worry. "What's going on, James?"

"I'm not sure, it's never done that before." I tried it again with the same result; nothing. "I guess I'll call the auto club and get a jump, must be a dead battery." Dean didn't look so convinced, he looked to the side and watched the last of the vehicles that had been here slowly leave the parking area.

"Can you make that call now? It's getting dark, and I don't know about you, but I don't want to find out if the stories about Dyer Lane are really about this place," Dean said.

I took out my phone and dialed the number, and at first nothing happened. I checked my phone a few times, and it seemed like we were out of a service area, which couldn't be, since we were still in town. I breathed a sigh of relief when it finally connected.

"Hello, how can I help you this evening?" a woman on the other end of the line asked.

"Hi, my car won't start, and we're in a somewhat rural area. We need someone to come out and get it started," I explained, being as patient as I could under the circumstances.

"Okay, let me see what I can do." I heard her tapping away on a keyboard. Dean was still looking out the window, and slowly turned to meet my eyes. He looked nervous, and I knew if I was worried about staying out here after dark, he was too. I reached over and took his hand, needing to feel his closeness. "What was that? I didn't catch what you said," I explained into the phone.

"Sir, unfortunately tonight is exceptionally busy, I can't get anyone out to your location for at least two hours. Will you be okay until then?" I considered her question for a second. Would we be okay? "I think so, we're in a parking lot so we're not on a street, but there's no one left out here, so I'd appreciate it if you could put a little speed into getting us out of here."

"I understand, sir, I'll see what I can do to expedite it. Give me your information and I'll call you back as soon as we can get someone to get out there to you." I gave her the information she requested, and when I hung up, Dean and I both sat there in silence, too much silence.

"James," he whispered, "this is really fucking creepy."

"I was thinking the same damn thing. What should we do? The auto club said they can't get out here for two hours at least. And with my luck it'll probably be four."

"What do we do now?" he asked.

"Now, we wait." We both sat there in silence for what seemed like forever but was probably only ten minutes. Finally, I couldn't take the quiet anymore, constantly waiting for something to happen. "So, Dean, can I ask you something?"

"Sure, anything," he said as he turned to face me.

"Are you really okay with the ghost thing? I mean, not many people would be. I know it's weird, and I know it's something that sounds fun until you're getting your ass kicked by a fucking spirit." He reached for my hand again, and held it between his own, reveling in his warmth. His closeness and calm demeanor were a balm to my frantic emotions.

"I'm okay with it. I'm not going to lie and say I understand it all, because I don't. But I'm not going anywhere, if that's what you're worried about. I'm in this with you, together."

"I'm so glad to hear you say that, I still feel bad about pushing you away before. I hope you understand, I thought I was keeping you safe."

"I know, I didn't like it, and if you ever do it again, I will kick your ass, but I understand why you did it. Even if I don't agree with your reasoning." He reached for me, and everything else faded into the background, there was only him and me. His lips were warm and soft, and his breaths came in rapid bursts as he kissed me until we both pulled apart to take a breath. Our eyes locked, and for a second, neither of us moved. I reached out my hand and glided my fingers through his hair, as a soft smile formed on his lips. "I love you, James," he said on a breath.

"I lo—" A scream tore through the silent night. It sounded so close, it startled us both and we jumped back against the seats. "What the fuck was that?" I asked, not really expecting an answer.

"James? Are we safe out here?" Dean asked, leaning forward to look out the windshield. A mist had settled over the pond we were parked close to. It drifted over the surface, and it seemed only a minute later it enveloped the whole area.

"Yeah, of course. Why wouldn't we be?"

"Well, maybe some of the ghosts from Dyer Lane decided to visit? How the fuck do I know? Should we call again and see how much longer for the tow truck?"

"She said she'd call back as soon as she had more information. I think we just need to wait." Dean leaned closer to the windshield and wiped at his eyes frantically.

"Are you okay?" I asked. He turned to face me, and the look on his face made my blood run cold. "What is it? What's wrong? Dean, are you okay?" His mouth opened and closed several times, but still no words came out. Finally he pointed toward the pond. I followed the direction he pointed and scanned the area. "What, Dean? What did you see?" I turned to face him again, and shook his arm, hoping to break the spell he seemed to be under. He shook his head and blinked his eyes. His mouth continued to open and close, but still no sound came out. I grabbed the front of his shirt and shook him. "Dean, for fuck's sake, what did you see?"

He cleared his throat before finally speaking. "I'm not sure, but I think I saw a woman out in the middle of the pond."

"What? How could that be? We're the only ones out here, and why would a woman be in the middle of the pond?"

"She was floating over it," he said, voice low and serious. "Gliding across it like it was iced over, then she just seemed to disappear into the fog, but before she did, she looked back this way. And I swear she met my eyes and waved at me to follow her. I thought you were the one the ghosts were drawn to, why would she be waving to me?"

"Ghosts suck, they don't do anything they're supposed to do. They do whatever the fuck they want. I have my power locked down, so she didn't see me. If she had, she would have been over here, trying to get to me, and probably you too." I dragged my hand down my face, I was sweating even though it was cold out. Fucking ghosts.

"What do we do?" he asked.

"Nothing, we wait here until the tow truck gets here, they start the car, and we get the hell out of here."

"Aren't you a little bit curious? What if she's lost and needs help?"

"What if she wants to hop into one of us and take a ride? How about that? Trust me, it sucks!"

"James," he said as he put his arm around my shoulder and squeezed my neck, silently urging me to relax. "Why don't you call Jason and see what he recommends? Maybe there's something we can do to help, or at least walk over that way and check if we see anything." He met my eyes, and I knew right then I was fucked. He had some weird power over me, and he seemed to know exactly how to use it.

"We'll walk over there and see what's going on. But we're not calling Jason, he'll want to come out here, and it'll be a full-on investigation before you can snap your fingers. He won't let up until he figures it out. Nope, no way, come on, let's go check it out." I opened the door and stepped outside the car, walked to the trunk, and took out the flashlight I had in my emergency kit—too bad it didn't include a jumpstart kit too. I walked around to where Dean stood by his door and reached out my hand. "Come on, let's get this over with." He smiled as he took my hand, and we walked across the empty dirt lot to the pond.

Chapter Four

The Pond

Dean

"Are you sure this is a good idea? I mean I know I insisted, but I have no clue how these things work. Should we call someone?" I babbled at James. He rolled his eyes and ignored me, but squeezed my hand as we walked toward the pond. When we reached the edge, we stopped, and he shined his flashlight around the area.

"Where did you see her?" he asked.

I looked around to get my bearings before I answered. "Right here. *Poof*, she appeared, then she walked out onto the water and disappeared." James listened to me, and once again shined his light around.

"I don't see anything, come on, let's go back to the car," he said.

I wasn't sure what it was I'd seen, at first I thought my eyes were playing tricks on me. She seemed to appear out of nowhere, not like the ghosts in the basement, more like I blinked and she was there. She turned to look right at me before walking on top of the pond and disappearing into the mist. Only I knew she wasn't gone. She wanted me to see her and follow her, but I was afraid to know why. James was the expert at ghosts, not me. Well, maybe not an expert, but he had experience—whether or not he liked it was another matter.

"No, let's go over to the other side, we can't see it very clearly through the mist. It won't take but a minute, and I promise we'll go right back to the car after." He considered it for a second and shined the flashlight in the direction I indicated we should go.

"Well, come on, then, let's get this over with. You really should hang out with Deidra, you two are both too persuasive for my own good."

We walked around the edge of the pond; it was pretty large, maybe the size of a football field or more. "This is where she disappeared," I said, looking at the ground and hoping to see footprints.

"I don't see anything," James said, and looked relieved. I scanned the area, as far as I could see with the mist that seemed to float in and out.

"What's that over there?" I said, seeing something white and glowing in the distance.

"Fuck, I was hoping we didn't see anything," James grumbled, but looked toward what appeared to be a glowing apparition.

"Do you see it?" I whispered as I gripped his arm. He gently pulled my fingers loose from his jacket and patted my hand on his arm.

"I see it, I'm not sure what it is, though. Can we go back to the car now?" He turned and tried to rush past me, but I caught his arm.

"James, what the fuck is that?" I whispered, afraid to make too much noise and draw attention to us. There, on the crest of a small rolling hill, were four white figures, they looked to be women with flowing white dresses that billowed in the mist. There were candles set all around them, and they seemed to be in the middle of some sort of ritual. All of them glowed from within, in a way that made it obvious they were not alive. We both froze and watched them. The slight breeze blew their voices to us; they were chanting something, and their voices were just low enough to make me want to listen, but not loud enough for me to make it out.

"James, what are they saying?" I glanced at him; he looked stricken. He wasn't exaggerating, he really didn't do well with ghosts. "Are you okay?" Before he could answer, the surrounding air changed. My breath was visible as it came out in panicked puffs, and I shivered uncontrollably. "James, what's happening?" I whispered. His eyes were wide with shock, and he panted out his breath as if he had just run here.

"They know we're here," he said, and grabbed my hand. He pulled me away from where we stood, and we broke into a run, headed for the car, as he dragged me behind him. But the mist encircled us.

"I can't see anything. Can you tell where the car is?" I asked.

"No, I can't see shit." James spun around, keeping his back to me as he faced off with whatever he seemed to think was coming at us from behind. "I know you're there, show yourself!" he shouted.

"Shh, James, don't let them know where we're at," I whispered.

"They already know, they're just fucking with us. Aren't you?" he yelled once again into the void the mist had created. "Come on, show yourself, you assholes. You think you're so tough when you're hiding behind the mist, let's see how tough you are face-to-face." He threw the challenge into the night, and I shrunk in behind him and clutched at his jacket. Why did I think this was a good idea again? "I knew you were here," I heard him say, and chanced a glance over his shoulder.

There stood four figures, they were blurry and looked more like a thick mist. None of them moved any closer to us, but they didn't retreat either. One of them shimmered, then and slowly formed into a shape that was more recognizable. It was a young woman, probably in her early twenties, with long brown hair that hung heavy around her shoulders. She wore a loose white dress that seemed to move as if it was part of her, and she was barefoot, which I thought for a moment was odd, then I realized it was all odd.

"What do you want?" James asked, pushing me to stay behind him.

At first, she said nothing, just stood there staring at him, then she smiled, and tilted her head. "James, I know of you. You've been very busy of late."

"What do you want?" he repeated, this time with a little more force.

"You know what I want, it's what we all want. To have our revenge on those who have wronged us."

"You realize the boys who hurt you all died. There's no one left for you to have revenge on." She slowly crept closer to us, I sucked in a startled breath, and felt James quiver at her close proximity. "Just leave, there's nothing for you here."

I felt him start to shake more violently, then something else began to happen. The air crackled around us, as though it was charged. "We need to go," I whispered to James.

"You can't go now," the spirit said, and in the blink of an eye, she was within inches of us.

"Fuck you, we can and we will," James shouted, and started to inch us back in what I hoped was the direction of the car, but the splash I heard forced me to stop, and stop him.

"The pond, she's forcing us toward the pond. Stop, James." I pounded on his shoulder, hoping to stop him pushing back against me. He reached back and pulled my hip closer to him, but didn't take his eyes off the spirit that seemed intent on harming us.

"Leave us alone, or you'll regret it, I'll send you back to wherever the hell you came from," James said, his voice a low growl.

She leaned in so close I could see her hair floating around her face, and I realized I could see right through her. Where her eyes should have been were dark hollows. I was transfixed by the horrific vision in front of me. When she realized I could see her from behind James, she moved to the side so I could see her completely. In that moment, I understood why James was so terrified.

"You have no power over me, my sisters and I are not like the other spirits you've dealt with. You have no protections that would harm us." She smiled, and it was the same as the other spirits in the basement—the look that said she knew way more than we did, and she was in control. "We will take the beacon from you, the amount of power it would give us would be considerable. Sadly, you won't survive."

James reached back and squeezed my hand, glancing back at me, then back to where the car was parked. "You're not taking nothing from me!" he yelled, and bolted toward the parking lot.

I paused for a second, but he jerked me close behind him, and we both ran as fast as we could. The mist broke for a few seconds, but then it was back, and once again preventing us from finding the car.

"What do we do?" I stayed as close to James as possible. We were both frantic to get away, tripping and falling over each other on the uneven ground. We must have been going the wrong direction, because suddenly there was a steep slope, and both of us tumbled down it. I expected to land in water, but instead it was just dirt and grass. It tore our hands apart as we tumbled, and when I finally came to a rest, I was alone. "James?" I whispered. No response. I stood and moved carefully around the area, not wanting to step on him if he'd been knocked unconscious by the fall. In the distance, another scream tore through the night, and I ducked and covered my head.

When I looked up again, I was surrounded by what was now a thick heavy fog, so thick I could barely make out my hand in front of my face. I took out my phone and shined it around the area. Even if James had been under my feet, I wouldn't have seen him. What the fuck had I gotten us into?

Chapter Five

The Witches

Jimbo

I must have been knocked out momentarily after we tumbled down the slope. I tried to jump up to my feet, but my head protested. Not again, the last thing I needed was another knock to the head.

"Dean?" I rolled onto my knees and sat back on my heels and listened. Nothing. "Dean?" I tried again, but somehow, I knew he couldn't hear me. I slowly stood and walked around a little, hoping I'd find him somewhere close, but a part of me knew I wouldn't. Then I heard footsteps, and they were walking toward me. I ducked down, not sure if it was Dean, and not wanting to find out the hard way that it was another ghost, or maybe something else they'd conjured up.

"Hey, mister, are you all right?" An older man with graying hair and wearing overalls walked up to me.

"Who are you?" I asked.

"I live around here, I saw your flashlight and thought I'd walk over and make sure you were okay. So, are you?"

"Do I look like I'm okay? Where's Dean?"

"What are you talking about, you're the only one I saw when I walked up? What are you doing here anyway?" the old man asked.

"We were here for the reenactment earlier, but my car wouldn't start." I stood and paused for a second, making sure I wasn't dizzy. "We were waiting for the auto club when we saw something over by the pond and came to check it out." I looked at the man's face, to see him staring at me like I'd lost my mind. "What? Why are you looking at me like that?"

"Mister, I have no idea what you're talking about. Auto club? Reenactment? What does all that mean anyway?"

"What the fuck are you talking about?" I looked around, still not able to see beyond the thick fog that had rolled in; it was as though he and I were the only ones in the world. "Where's Dean? Dean?" I cupped my hands and yelled into the fog while I walked back up to the top of the embankment we'd fallen down. "Dude, where the hell is Dean? Did you see him when you walked over here? And where the hell did you walk from? There's nothing around here." I turned back to look at him, only to find him gone too.

"What the—" I spun around, just in time to see the four shapes we'd seen before. Only now they didn't appear as hazy forms. I could see all four women clearly, moving around what appeared to be an altar area, and involved in what looked like some kind of ritual. One of them chanted something the other three repeated back to her, and then all of them went about their part of whatever it was they were involved in. Time seemed to stand still, and all of them turned to look right at me.

"James, we've been waiting for you," one of them said, and motioned for me to go to her. I shook my head and backed away, but started to slide down the embankment again. The four of them moved toward me, each of them holding something in their hands. As they got closer, they spread out and surrounded me. If I went backward, I'd be at the bottom of the embankment again, with nowhere to go.

"Why are you here? There's nothing I'm willing to give you, now just back off."

"We're where we should be, it was prophesied that you'd be here at this time on this night, and here you are. Now we can use your power for the ritual we need to keep our spirits alive in another witch's body forever, and continue our goal of maintaining the power of our coven," one of them explained. She was different from the one Dean and I had seen earlier.

"You're not using my power for anything, it's not up for discussion, thank you very much. Now I'll just be leaving, if you don't mind."

"No, James, you won't." They moved faster than I could move to avoid them, coming at me from all sides at once. I started to stumble back again at their advance, but two of them grabbed my arms, while the other one slipped a rope around first one wrist, then the other.

"Fuck, what are you doing? I don't want any trouble with you, leave me the hell alone." I struggled with them as they secured my wrists. They all worked together to drag me toward a big oak tree they had drawn symbols on I didn't understand or recognize.

"As you can see, we were all prepared for you. Now don't worry, we won't kill you on purpose, but we will take your power, and you may not survive it," the one that seemed to be in charge explained. She was so sure of herself, as though she knew without a doubt they wouldn't fail, and maybe she was right, but I wouldn't go down without a fight. I struggled with the ropes, but the harder I pulled, the more it hurt and the tighter they felt. "The more you struggle, the more it will fight to hold you. If you relax, it will loosen, but it will not let you go free. Such a simple but useful spell, wouldn't you agree?"

My chest heaved as I tried to control my emotions and not panic, but I could feel it rising in me, and eventually they'd get what they wanted. I'd lose control of my power and either call up spirits I had no desire to deal with, or they'd take my power. "How are you here? Before you were a spirit, now you're solid. How?"

They all stopped whatever they were doing to prepare for the ritual I wanted no part of. "Did you not understand what has happened? We brought you to us. We folded time, so we could bring you here with us." The one in charge moved closer to me. "You're very valuable to us, James, it was risky for us to bring you here, but it will be worth it in the end."

What the fuck? I looked around; the area was still engulfed in fog, so all that was visible was the little clearing Dean and I had seen their spirits in. "How can you have brought me back? That's impossible."

"Oh sweet James, did your sister not inform you of all the many ways we can use nature to do our bidding?" another of the witches said.

"Sister, come, we need to prepare the fire for the final part of the ritual." The one that had been talking to me walked over to join the other three, and they all helped start a small fire. Next they put a pot on it, and each of them added the different items they'd been holding earlier. Some of it I recognized as herbs or flowers, but some of it was unfamiliar to me.

When it seemed they'd mixed everything into the pot, they all stood, and reached out for one another's hands. They slowly walked around the fire in a clockwise motion while chanting something I didn't understand. Each of them carried a branch of some plant or tree, I wasn't sure.

"James," I thought I heard someone say from behind me, but how could that be? This whole situation was hopeless. No one could help me now, I was fucked. "James, it's me, Dean," he whispered, his voice tight and frantic.

"Dean?" I had to be hallucinating. Maybe they'd hexed me, or slipped me some hallucinogen without me knowing? Or maybe this time, this one time, I'd be lucky. At least lucky enough to get out of here.

Chapter Six

Caught

Dean

One minute we were falling down an embankment as we tried to run away from what appeared to be the spirit of a witch, and then I found myself alone. I wasn't sure what had happened to James, or myself.

I rolled to my side and tried to get my feet under me so I could stand, but I was disoriented, my head swimming as I clutched it in my hands. Finally I was able to look up, and I realized I had ended up at the bottom of the embankment we'd tumbled down.

"James?" I didn't move and listened so hard my ears hurt. But I heard nothing. "James, can you hear me?" I tried again, this time a little louder. Again no reply. I crouched down and made my way to the top of the embankment; the fog wasn't as thick as it had been, but I still couldn't see very far. I stumbled around in the dark but didn't want to get too far away in case James was close by and injured. I called his name again—still got no answer. I could make out the pond, and some trees in close proximity, but I didn't see anyone around. I stood there for a second longer, trying to figure out what I should do. I took out my phone, but it had no signal. Great, it had been fine earlier, now when I needed it . . .

Movement to my left caught my eye, and I could just make out four shapes in white. I started to move toward them, not knowing what else to do, and tried to be as quiet as possible. I moved around to the side of them and stayed in the tree line. From here I could see it was four women, all dressed in long, flowing white dresses. They all seemed to move around an area that looked like an altar, each of them carrying something in their hands, but I wasn't close enough to see what it was.

I continued through the edge of the clearing, ducking behind oak trees, and hoping they didn't see me. Finally I was just behind where they were standing. They each took turns putting something in a metal pot they'd placed over a fire. I could hear them chanting, but once again I couldn't make out what they were saying. I leaned against the tree and tried to peek around it to see what they were doing now. Then I heard it, a shuffling sound at the opposite side of the tree. I peered around the trunk and saw a blue jacket, the same blue jacket James had on. "James?" I whispered, hoping the sound didn't carry past him.

"Dean?" I heard the ropes rub against the tree as he struggled with them.

"Shh, don't move, I'm going to try to get closer to you without them seeing."

"Be careful, they want to use me in their ritual and take my power," he whispered back to me. I slid around the side of the tree until I could see where they'd tied him up. I tried to reach around and untie him but wasn't having much luck.

"James, do you have a knife on you? I can't untie you from here."

"Dean, if I had a fucking knife, how would I give it to you with my fucking hands tied?" he whisper-yelled, sounding more and more afraid and frustrated by the second.

"Right, right, sorry. Okay, I'm going to move around to the side and see if I can get it from there."

"Be careful, Dean," he whispered. I slid to the side and stayed low to the ground, trying to use the surrounding grass to stay concealed.

"Well, what have we here?" a woman's voice said from right behind me. I turned and tried to scurry away from where I thought she was, but she grabbed my arm and held me tight. "You must be a friend of James's. Why don't you join him? The more the merrier, we can always use more blood for our incantation, it'll make it that much stronger." She shoved me back against the tree, and her strength surprised me.

"Who are you and what do you want from us?" I asked as she tied me next to James. In a flash, I thought back to how much we'd already been through, how much *he'd* been through, and I knew I couldn't stand here and do nothing. I shoved her back from me, and she stumbled and fell. I used that split second to slip the rope off my hand that she hadn't had time to tighten.

"Sisters, come help," she said as she stumbled to her feet. I worked at the rope on James's wrist, and finally freed it just as she came rushing back at us again. I shoved her back and moved to undo his other hand.

"You won't get away, James, we will use your power as we intended," another one said as she rushed to help the woman that had grabbed me.

"Come on, Dean, let's get out of here," James said, his voice sounding more and more frantic. The rope slipped from his wrist, and I gripped his hand. We ran as fast as we could from the clearing, not knowing if we'd be able to outrun them or not. I heard the footfalls of the women right on our heels, but I didn't look back, I ran as fast as I could back in the direction I'd come.

"Dean. Dean!" James yelled. I slid to a stop and pulled him behind me as I spun around to look back. I expected to see the women chasing us, but there was nothing. The fog had thickened again and made it impossible for me to see if anyone was close by. I wasn't taking any chances, though.

"Where are they? They were right behind us?" I asked, spinning around again to make sure they hadn't somehow gotten in front of us.

"I see you found your friend." I spun back around at the sound of an unfamiliar voice. James was as startled as I was and jumped so hard, he jerked on my hand. "Whoa, sorry there. Didn't mean to scare you." A gray-haired man wearing overalls stood just to the edge of the embankment that dropped off into the pond.

"Oh hey, mister, yeah. Well actually, he found me," James said, and stepped around me with his hand extended. "There were a few women in the clearing over there, you didn't see them, did you?"

The man looked at his hand for a second before he shook it and looked over his shoulder in the direction James had indicated. "The clearing at the edge of the trees? You should stay away from there, it's not safe."

"Yeah, we found that out. Some women tied up James, then tried to tie me up too. I'm not sure what they wanted us for, or who they are," I said, looking at James.

"They're witches, they died here many years ago. But they come back every once in a while and try to take out some revenge on any unsuspecting person they happen upon. You two got lucky," the old guy said.

"Are you saying what I think you're saying? Ghosts took James?"

"No, they weren't ghosts, they were real. Somehow, they were real," James said.

"Son, they've been dead close to a hundred years, there's no way you saw anyone other than a ghost."

"I'm telling you, I was right there with them for a while. They were real, they had some ritual they wanted to perform so they could change their outcome and get some other power, they were real," James insisted.

"I saw them too, one of them grabbed my arm, and she was real." I looked at the man, and something didn't look quite right. I couldn't put my finger on what it was, but I knew it was time for James and I to get the hell out of here. "Let's get back to the car, the auto club should be here anytime now." I tugged on James's hand and moved to go to the parking lot.

"What did you see?" he asked the man, not moving at all.

"Well, I didn't see anything. I saw you two walking back this way after I'd talked to you earlier."

"Where did you disappear to when I was looking for Dean?"

The man didn't answer, just smiled, turned around, and started walking away. James looked at me and then back to where he was walking. As he moved away from us, the fog swallowed him, so he was hidden once again.

"Let's go wait in the car, I can't take much more of this weird shit," I said to James.

"I totally agree," he said, and pulled me along behind him. We made our way over the rough ground until we were finally at the edge of the parking lot. The fog was still heavy, and I couldn't see our car.

"Do you know where we parked?" I asked.

"Yeah, it's over this way. I can't believe we got stuck out here in the middle of the fucking night. Something's not right around here," James mumbled as we walked along.

"What's that?" I asked, for what felt like the hundredth time tonight. James stopped walking and looked in the direction I pointed. Four shapes floated just off the ground in front of us. James stopped short and stared at them.

"Fuck, they found us," he said, and rushed to back away from them.

"James, what—"

Chapter Seven

Ritual

Jimbo

They had found us again. "Dean, don't stop, we need to get the fuck out of here," I yelled back to him as I hauled ass over the rough terrain. I wasn't sure where we should go, but we needed to get away from them. I still held Dean's hand, and no way in hell was I letting go.

We ran until I couldn't run anymore, and I could feel Dean pulling his hand back, trying to get me to let go. "Wait, I can't run any farther. What's going on? I don't understand any of this." I stopped but didn't let go of him.

"They'll take my power, Dean. I always thought I'd be happy to get rid of it, but I know if they take it, they'll use it to destroy the world as we know it." I knew I was rambling, but I couldn't shut it down. I was shitting myself in fear of what I knew would happen if we didn't get away from them. "They'll use you too, they'll do whatever it takes to get what they want."

"But they're not real, James. It had to be some dream or illusion we saw. I'm not sure what it was, but it can't have been real."

I took him by the shoulders and shook him. "It was real, they told me they bent time and brought us back to when they were still alive, so they could take my power. They mean to take it no matter what, and being ghosts won't stop them. They're witches, Dean, honest-to-god witches. And they will fuck us up." He stood and stared at me with his mouth hanging open in obvious shock. "We have to get away from them," I said, trying to sound a little less crazy.

"James, where do we go? I have no clue where we are, do you?"

"No, I haven't been to this park in years, and I didn't exactly wander around all over it." I took my phone out and checked for a signal—one bar, but worth a try. I dialed and held the phone up to my ear, waiting for it to connect.

"Jimbo, what the fuck are you doing calling us this late?" Jason's voice seemed too loud in the silent night.

"Quiet, Jason, we're so fucked. You have to come out here and help us. I don't know what to do, and Dean and I are in some real shit." I heard him shuffle around, and then I heard him wake up Wade.

"What's going on?" he asked, sliding into full ghost hunter mode in an instant.

"We came out to watch a reenactment and—" Dean ripped the phone away from me before I could say another word.

"Jason, some fucking witch ghosts are chasing us all over the damn place, we don't know what to do. The car won't start so we're stuck, they caught James once and took us back in time, and now they want to take James's power and possibly use my blood for some freaky ritual. This is a nine-one-one situation, get your asses out here now!" He pulled the phone away from his ear and looked at it, then at me, then back at the phone.

"What did he say?" I asked.

"Nothing, not a goddamn thing, I think I lost him," Dean whispered, putting the phone to his ear again, and jumping when Jason answered.

"You didn't lose me, but it sounds like you are losing your shit, you need to calm down. Let me talk to Jimbo." I could hear Jason through the phone and took it from Dean, who stood with eyes wide as he handed it to me.

"Jason, we really need help, we're not safe here."

"Okay, it'll take us a good thirty minutes to get there, so just hang tight. You say they're ghosts of witches?"

"Yes, well, at least that's what one told me when they had me tied up. That they were witches and needed my power and would use it to maintain the power of their coven by putting their spirits into another witch's body."

"Fuck, okay, I'm going to grab a few things I think will help and we'll haul ass there."

"Thanks, man, I wasn't sure what else to do, and we've been running around and hiding for a while now."

"Well keep hiding, maybe get to a place where you're safe and can observe them without them seeing you," Jason instructed.

"What do you think we were doing? We tried to avoid them completely, and they did some time travel shit and put us right in the middle of it, we had no control over what happened at all."

"Jimbo, go hide, find a safe place and you and Dean stay put. We'll hurry and be there as soon as we can." I hung up and met Dean's eyes. He was scared, and I was right there with him. I knew I should try to be strong, but I didn't have it in me.

"Let's go, we'll see if we can find some cover for the time being. Hopefully Jason and Wade get here fast." Dean took my hand, and we trotted over to an area on the edge of the park that was less maintained and growing wild. The bushes and branches grabbed at our clothes and made it hard to walk without getting tangled in them. After walking through enough star thistle to last me the rest of my life, we found a cement culvert and a pipe big enough for us to both fit in it. "This looks good, they won't think to look here." I sounded more confident than I felt, as I jumped down to the dry creek bed and Dean followed.

I walked to the edge of the pipe and peered in, I couldn't see much of anything. I realized I no longer had my light with me, it was back at the clearing the witches had been in. Not wanting to turn my phone on for fear it would give us away, I stepped a little ways into the big pipe. I could stand in it if I ducked my head, and I was happy we wouldn't have to lie down in it to hide.

"Dean, we'll sit here until we hear from Jason, they'll be here soon. We should be safe." He followed me in and we both slid down the pipe to squat facing toward the entrance, squeezed close enough together I could feel him from my shoulder down to my knee.

"What do we do if they come here looking for us again?"

"We run. We can't fight them, they're different. I think they can still do spells, or whatever the fuck witches do. I'm pretty sure they can still do it. They used a spell on the rope that held me, to make it tighten if I tried to escape. They won't hold back this time if they get the chance to get what they want." He shook as he sat next to me. This wonderful man, who was for some reason willing to put up with me, had been thrown into so much shit in the short time we'd been together. I put my arm around him and pulled him as close as I could. "I'm so sorry, I wanted us to go somewhere different and have a fun date. I always loved coming to different fall events, and I thought this was a little more adult than taking you to a pumpkin patch." I was such an idiot. After this, Dean would never want to see me again. I rubbed my forehead against his temple, hoping this wasn't the last time we had together.

He leaned closer to me and wrapped both his arms around my waist. "Whatever you're thinking in that thick skull of yours, stop it. You couldn't have known any of this would happen. I love that you thought of something different, and walking around this beautiful park with you all day was one of the best days I've had in a while. I meant what I said earlier, I love you, James Collins, never doubt that. I'm in this with you all the way, you won't be getting rid of me quite so easy."

"I'm the luckiest motherfucker there is," I said as the lump in my throat threatened to choke me. I pulled him in even closer, and my eyes closed as I breathed in his fresh, clean scent. "We should have gone to a pumpkin patch."

"Oh, we're going, maybe next week?" he said, and turned enough to cup my cheek. "We're so going." He kissed me as hard as he could, given that we were both squeezed close side by side in a drainage pipe. And something in that kiss made me believe everything he'd said—I knew we could make it work, and it would be great. I pulled back enough to meet his eyes, while his thumb traced my cheek.

"I love you, Dean. I know I don't say it enough, and I'm sorry about that. It's on my list of things to do better. You always were it for me." He met my eyes, and didn't look away, not even for a second. A soft smile formed on his lips at my words, and if it hadn't been so dark in that pipe, I'd have seen him blush. "I love you," I repeated. My hand reached up and covered his that still rested against my cheek.

"Let's do this, let's kick these witches asses. Or whatever it takes to get the hell out of here."

"Slow down there, tiger, we need to wait for Wade and Jason, they'll know what to do. They always know what to do." And that's what we did. It seemed to take forever and fly by too. From our hiding place, we saw the fog roll in and cover the area even thicker. The temperature seemed to fall, and since we were sitting in a metal pipe, we had no insulation from the cold. Dean shivered, and all we could do was try to sit as close as possible and wait it out. We whispered to each other things we'd said many times before, and things we'd both held back. I realized we learned more about each other in the time we'd been here than we had all the nights we'd spent together so far.

"I think we need to make this an annual tradition," Dean said.

"Sitting in a drainpipe, hiding from witches?" I asked. "Because I'm not sure I can handle this every year." He shoved me hard, making me almost fall over before I caught myself. We both held back a laugh, and it felt so fucking good, it made my eyes tingle with unshed happy tears.

"Jimbo! What the hell are you guys doing hiding in here?" Jason seemed to appear out of nowhere and scared the hell out of both of us.

"Jason, oh my god, I'm so glad you guys are here. I'll forgive the fact that you almost gave me a heart attack." I moved to the entrance of the pipe, pulling Dean along behind me. "Where's Wade?"

"He's at the car. You guys ready to see what we can find out?"

"Jason, we need to get back to Wade, he's not safe there." Jason turned and bolted away from us. Dean and I hopped out of the drainpipe and watched him as he disappeared into the fog. "Let's go, they need us," I said, and both of us followed in the direction Jason had run. I hoped it wasn't a mistake, and I wasn't leading Dean into even more trouble, but either way, we'd know soon.

Chapter Eight

The Rescue

Dean

"I had no clue Jason could run that fast," I said to James as we tried to keep up.

"Less talking, more running," he replied, and pulled me along behind him. I kept thinking back to the conversation Jason had interrupted. I couldn't believe he really thought something like this would make me leave him.

"You're stuck with me, you know," I said, just because I wanted to say the words. He looked over his shoulder and smiled at me before picking up speed and dragging me along. We made it to the car much faster than we'd made it to the pipe, after tripping over a few rocks and getting scratched by some star thistle. Fucking star thistle.

"Jason? Is everything okay?" James asked as we got closer to their car. It was running and the parking lights were on, something I was thankful for since it had been so dark out here without it. Jason stepped away from the car, and Wade followed him.

"Everything's fine, it worried me he was alone out here. I thought I could run ahead and get you guys then come right back, but you were farther away than I thought," Jason explained.

"How'd you find us anyway?" I asked.

"Oh, we put a tracking app on our phones in case we ever got separated. I guess we know it works, if it could find you in a freaking drainpipe. What were you even doing in there?" Wade asked.

"We have been getting chased all damn night by fucking witches. When they came after us in the parking lot, I didn't want to take any chances, so we ducked in the drainpipe," James said.

"Witches? So I googled this area, and there used to be a coven around here, but that was close to a hundred years ago," Jason said.

"Yeah, these have been dead for a while, something happened to them, they're looking to reform their coven and get a little revenge. And not just on the people that did them wrong," James explained.

"What exactly did they tell you?" Jason asked.

"They said they could take my power from me and use Dean's blood, in some ritual that would make them able to put their spirits in another witch, and using my powers, they could bring back their coven and strengthen it more than before. Then they could do what they've always intended. I'm not sure of all the details, I was too busy trying to figure a way to escape to pay too much attention to what they were saying. Luckily Dean showed up and helped me get away," James said.

"Why didn't you just leave?" Wade asked.

"We've been trying to leave for hours, asshole. My car won't start, I told you I called the auto club, and they still aren't here. I don't know what the holdup is."

"Maybe somehow the spirits aren't letting you leave. Did you think of that? If they want you here for a reason, they could be forcing you to stay," Jason said; his knowledge of all things to do with ghosts was a little creepy.

"Oh, they want us here for a reason, I told you that. We've been running from them all damn night. And some old dude showed up, he did nothing at all to help. Just talked a bit and then disappeared, said he lived around here somewhere. I'm not sure why he didn't offer to give us a jump," James continued, as Jason and Wade leaned against their car.

"So what do we do now?" I asked. "Is it even possible to force a witch to move on? Why would they want to if they still have so much power over the living?"

"It's possible, and I think I have just what we need. I did a little research, and apparently they used to use a common object to keep houses safe from witches, around the same time as the Salem witch trials. It doesn't seem like it could work, but I've got nothing else. If they are witches, then it will be harder to get them to pass over. Hopefully this helps us convince them it's time to go," Jason said as he patted his backpack.

"What exactly did you bring?" James asked.

"You'll see. Now, show us where they had you tied up, maybe that's where they're bound to," Jason added.

"Are you sure that'll work? It sounds a little too simple, and what do we do if it doesn't?" Wade asked, stepping closer to Jason and wrapping his arms around his waist.

"If it doesn't work, we'll try to cross them over anyway, and see how it goes. If that doesn't work, we'll have to do more research and come back. But we're out of options. There's not a lot written about ghosts of witches and how to get rid of them," Jason answered.

"Let's get this over with," James said, and squeezed my hand before leading us toward the pond again. "This is where it all started, Dean saw what looked like a woman out in the pond, only she wasn't in the water, she was floating above it. We followed, and that's where all the shit started."

As we all walked along, Jason took out a couple of their gadgets, and he and Wade waved them around as we went. Neither device made much noise, so I took that as a good sign.

"So, car wouldn't start, huh?" Wade said, smirking at James and I.

"Fuck you, Wade, I can be alone with Dean anytime I want and not be freezing my ass off while avoiding ghosts who want to put a hex on us." He squeezed my hand tighter, and I pulled him closer to me.

"You can be alone with me anytime you want," I said, and gripped his arm with my free hand.

"Oh god, you two have it bad. My mom will have a field day with this. You might want to tone that down when you see her next time, Jimbo," Wade said, and Jason shoved him. They both laughed and continued waving their devices around. Suddenly one of them started beeping, not a slow irregular beep, but more like a warning.

"What does that mean?" I asked.

"It means things are about to get interesting," Jason replied.

"It means we're all going to regret coming back here," James said, and pulled me even closer. We creeped up to the edge of the pond, and the beeping sounded faster and louder before it cut off completely, throwing us into complete silence. Across the pond, a bright point appeared. It grew until it was big enough for us to see clearly that it was a woman, all dressed in white. She seemed to look in our direction and floated toward us across the pond.

"Is that what you saw earlier?" Wade asked.

"Yep," I said, in a very self-satisfied way.

"Well fuck," Jason said, before the flashlights and devices died completely and we were once again plunged into darkness.

Chapter Nine

Witch Ball

Jimbo

The closer we got the pond, the more convinced I was this was a bad idea. Jason didn't sound all that confident in whatever it was he had planned working. As we stepped up to the edge of the pond, everything died down, all sound and all light were suddenly gone. I felt Dean tense next to me and cursed the fact I'd once again put him in danger.

"Okay, guys, how far is the clearing from here?" Jason asked, back in ghost hunter mode.

"It's probably a hundred yards past the pond. It's surrounded by a grove of oak trees, so if you didn't know it was there, you'd probably miss it," Dean said, and added, "I only saw it because I caught sight of the fire they had set and noticed movement, otherwise I wouldn't have had any idea it was there."

The spirit continued to glide toward us, though she seemed to avoid getting too close; maybe she knew whatever Jason had with him could hurt her. Suddenly she rushed up to us, her face now transformed. Her jaw hung loose and gaping, and her eyes bulged from her skull as she appeared more as a corpse than a living person now.

Wade flinched back from her, and Jason stepped between them. "Back the fuck off," he yelled. He rummaged in his backpack without taking his eyes off the spirit who was practically nose to nose with him and pulled out a heavy glass orb. He thrust it out in front of him, and before the spirit could react, he plunged it into her chest.

She screamed and flinched away from it. "What have you done? What have you done?" she screamed over and over.

"Witch ball, bitch. I just took all your powers away. If you know what's good for you, you'll do as I say and leave," Jason yelled over her screams.

"You won't defeat my sisters. We will destroy you, and we'll use your friend's power to change our destiny."

"No, you won't, he's one of us and we stick together. Now leave, you're not welcome here," Jason yelled again, and she started to fade. All at once, she seemed to glow brighter, and then she released a scream I felt in my bones and that made the ground shake.

And then she was gone.

Jason turned around and tucked the witch ball away into his backpack. He rubbed his hands together and kissed Wade on the side of the head. "Okay, let's go get the rest of them," he said, and wove his fingers with Wade's and walked toward the clearing.

Wade looked back at the two of us. "You two coming?"

Dean and I looked at each other before scrambling to keep up with them. We walked into the area where the trees seemed to block out everything around them, shielding us from the outside world. It was creepy as hell, but that didn't stop Wade and Jason from marching right into the unknown.

"Can you show us where were you tied up?" Jason asked. I stopped and looked around for a moment, and Dean did the same.

"It's hard to say for certain, it was dark and foggy, like it is now."

"It was right over there," Dean said, pointing to a tree that grew right at the edge of what I could now see was a big clearing. "They tied him to the side facing into the clearing, when they caught me, they tied me to this side, or they tried. We got away from them, but barely."

"Everyone, stay together, and keep your voices down. We don't want to alert them to us being here," Jason said, afraid to bring attention to us. We all crept closer to the tree, no one saying a word. We found the tree with the ropes still clinging to it where we'd left them. I walked up to it and put my hand on the rough bark, and my finger traced partially over one of the many symbols they'd drawn.

"This is it," I whispered to Jason. He nodded his understanding and slunk closer. He leaned around the trunk and tried to look at the clearing, then stiffened and ducked back behind the tree, his eyes wide and his hands braced behind him. "What did you see?" Wade moved closer to Jason.

"They're in the clearing, they've made a fire, and it looks like they're getting ready for something," Jason said.

"How many are there?" Wade asked.

"Three, there are three. I wish I had time to translate some of these symbols, they might give us a clue to how to stop them."

"Babe, the witch ball worked. We got this," Wade said.

"Yeah, we have to get each of them to touch the ball, this'll be great," I said. *Why couldn't it ever be easy?*

"We can do it, James, we'll all work together again," Dean said. Damn, why'd he have to be so sweet and look at me like that? I smiled despite myself, and when I looked at Wade, he covered his mouth to stifle a laugh.

"Fuck you, Wade, let's do this," I said. I grabbed Dean's hand and stepped closer to Wade and Jason. "What's your plan?" Jason explained his idea; it was simple, and I hoped it worked. There was only one problem I had with it—I'd be the bait.

"Just stand at the base of the tree until one of them sees you, then dart back here. When she gets close, I'll touch her with the ball. Easy peasy," Jason said. Wade looked at him and smiled. I couldn't control my eye roll. They had it so bad.

"You really think that'll work? What if all three of them decide to follow me?"

"Then we'll get creative and touch all three," Wade said.

"I feel so much better hearing you say that." I rolled my eyes again and squeezed Dean's hand before letting it go. "Let's get it over with." I stepped around the tree, and as soon as I did, all three of the spirits looked up and rushed over toward us.

"Where is our sister? What have you done?" they screeched. I moved, just like Jason had told me to do, but suddenly I was frozen, my feet felt as though they were stuck to the ground. My eyes met Dean's, and I saw my shock reflected in his own before I was tugged back out from behind the tree and pulled into the clearing.

"You will help us one way or another, I can promise you that," one of the witches said, as they held me dangling just above the ground and unable to move. I noticed movement behind the trees, and my eyes once again found Dean's, and I knew we were really screwed now. Dean rushed out toward me faster than I'd ever seen him move. He slammed into me, and the force knocked him back onto the ground. I still couldn't move; all I could do was watch helplessly as he became the witches' next victim.

Chapter Ten

Not Running Scared

Dean

The force of hitting James stunned me for a moment. I slammed to the ground, and by the time I knew what was going on one of the witches had come closer to me. She leaned down into my face and opened her mouth to speak, but before she did, I scrambled to get the ball out of my pocket. It was a tight fit in my jacket pocket, and I struggled with it for a second before finally pulling it free, just as she was inches from me. I shoved it toward her and touched her.

At first, she seemed to not realize what had happened, she still loomed over me as I scrambled to put some distance between us. "You cannot hurt me, human, I have more powers than you will ever imagine," she bragged, and her skeletal features became more visible. Then something changed, and she seemed to realize she wasn't as strong as she had boasted. Jason ran out from behind the tree and commanded her to cross over. He and Wade watched as the same thing happened with this witch that had with the first as soon as she was without her magic—she had no power to stay here any longer. She seemed to realize this at the same time we did, and as she screamed out her rage then disappeared, I realized two were now gone.

But two more remained, and we'd pissed them off. I turned to face the clearing again, and both of them were right behind us, hands curled into claws and looking even more horrible than before.

"James," I yelled, and rushed over to help him up and put some distance between us and the spirits. Jason rushed forward and held out a crystal. The spirits looked at it as if it were nothing.

"Your crystals will not work on us, where did you get a witch ball? You will not have the same success with the two of us," one spirit screamed at Jason.

"It will, and you know it will," Jason said in a calm voice. The spirits glided back and forth before us; and kept us pinned to the tree but didn't move to do more. They seemed scared of what they knew would happen.

"Cross over, and we won't use the witch ball," Wade said. "I know you're afraid of what will happen to you if we use it, but you have to leave this place, you're not welcome here anymore. You've done enough harm while you've been here."

"What of the other spirits? Do they not need to leave also?" the other witch asked.

"You planned to use two of our friends, to take their power and their lives for a ritual that would have brought you more power. You need to leave. You're evil, and if you don't cross over, we'll make you," Jason said.

"We are not the only spirits that could harm you. They have left us in limbo for years, we only wanted to complete the spell that would set us free," the spirit said in a soft, soothing voice.

"You're lying," Wade spoke up. "You didn't have to do this, you could have crossed over on your own years ago, but you stayed here hoping to have a chance at revenge and power."

"You know nothing," the other spirit boomed out as she rushed up to Wade. Jason jumped between them and held out the witch ball I'd passed back to him. She looked right at it before backing off.

"It's your choice, either go willingly or we'll make you," Jason said. He still held the witch ball out to them. In an instant, the one who had been farther away rushed at him. Jason didn't flinch; he held the ball out and plunged it into her chest as her hands reached out, trying to grasp him. She instantly stopped, and her head turned to look at her companion before she faded out of existence.

Wade stepped closer to the remaining spirit. "You know there's nothing you can do, this all ends here. I understand your pain at losing your sisters, but you'll all be together again on the other side of the veil. Your pain and suffering will end. Now please, go willingly, don't make us do the same to you as we have to your sisters. This way your magic will stay with you when you join them. Go, I won't give you another chance." He glanced to his left where Jason stood holding the witch ball. The spirit looked between them and slowly began to fade.

"You won't hear from us again, we will all be together and free," she said, before disappearing into nothing. The air seemed lighter, the night not as heavy as it had a few moments before. The fog that had been clinging to us all night lifted. I looked up, and the stars were out, it was beautiful.

"Jimbo, you want a jump?" Wade asked. "We brought the jumper cables."

"Yeah, man, let me call and cancel the auto club." He pulled out his phone and redialed the number, since they had yet to show up, there wasn't an issue.

Wade looked over at me and smiled as he took Jason's hand. "That was crazy, huh? I've never heard of a ghost that's still a witch." He leaned up and kissed Jason on the cheek.

"Oh, young one, there is so much I will teach you," Jason said as he threw his arm around Wade's shoulders and pulled him close to kiss the side of his head. I looked over at James and caught him mid eye roll. He looked over at me and winked, I knew exactly what he was thinking. Wade and Jason were just so into each other when they were together. He wanted to hate it, but deep inside he thought it was the cutest thing ever, and the smile he was fighting to conceal proved it.

We all walked over to the cars, and Jason took out his go bag that held anything we'd ever need, and after connecting the batteries, James's car started right up.

"You guys leave when we do, I don't want to have to come back again," Jason said as he coiled up the jumper cables and put them back into his trunk.

"Don't worry, we don't want to be here any longer than necessary." James and I got into the car and followed Jason and Wade as they led us out of the parking lot.

"Did you see that?" I asked, pointing across the road we were driving on, which led to the main road.

"See what?" James said as he looked out my window.

"I saw that old guy, he was waving to us."

"The farmer?"

"Yes. Do you think maybe he—no, never mind, I don't even want to know. Let's get home." He took my hand and pulled it into his lap.

"I'm ready for home too." We followed Wade and Jason until we got to the I-80 on-ramp where we lost them. James drove us to my house, which had become our usual routine. I'd yet to spend the night at his house, but it didn't matter, as long as we were together each night, everything was right.

Epilogue

Dean

After a very long night, we finally pulled into the driveway of the house we now pretty much shared. I knew James loved his place in Coloma, but I was selfish, I wanted him with me all the time.

"What's going on in that beautiful mind?" James asked as he turned off the car and stepped out.

"Just wondering how long you'll keep denying you live here . . . with me," I said, trying to sound as casual about it as I could, but from the look on his face, failing horribly.

He stepped close to me as we met behind the car and cupped my jaw in both his warm hands. "Is that what you really want? Because I want it so bad, but I've been making myself not ask you. I was too afraid you'd say no," James said, his brows pinched in concern.

I reached up and cupped his face, too, and brushed my thumb over his ear. "How could you ever think I'd want any less? I love you, James, I won't ever want anyone else the way I want you. I think loving you all these years is why I've always been single. My heart was waiting for its other half." His eyes grew a little brighter, and a tear threatened to spill over his lashes, but he smiled instead.

"Dean, I love you, I know for a fact there is not another person in the world who would put up with the shit you have tonight, and not be running for the hills. You deserve to know how much you mean to me, and how special you are, every day. And I plan to spend every moment of every day doing just that. You're everything to me, you're that special person I never thought I'd find. And when I met you and knew I couldn't have you, I never forgot. I never wanted anyone who didn't make me feel the way you did all those years ago. And no one ever has, except you. I love you, I love you with every part of my heart. And I really am sorry I was so stupid and waited so long to tell you that, or to even contact you. It's one of my biggest regrets." Now it was my eyes that felt a little too wet, and I struggled to hold back the emotion that nearly strangled me, as he punctuated every "I love you" with a kiss.

I wrapped my arms around him at the same time he pulled me impossibly closer to him. "I love you, please move in with me," I begged. I wasn't ashamed of how much I wanted him, and I wouldn't hide it.

He pressed his face into my neck and inhaled deeply before nodding. "There's nothing else I want more. Now the only thing we have to do is probably the most dangerous," James said as he pulled back enough to look me in the eye. He brushed his thumbs underneath my eyes, collecting the moisture gathered there.

"What are you talking about? What could be worse than being stranded with the ghosts of four witches?" I asked.

"Deidra. As soon as I tell her I'm moving in with you, there'll be a rip in the space-time continuum when she screams her head off. Be prepared, Dean, you have no clue what you're in for," James said, his voice serious, but his eyes alight with humor.

"I can handle Deidra," I said, before I kissed him. "Right now I really need to feel your skin on mine, and forget about all the weird shit that happened tonight."

"That sounds like the best idea I've heard tonight, let's get inside before your neighbors think we're up to no good."

"We are up to no good." I took his hand, and we stumbled in the door, barely taking the time to unlock it. He shoved me up against the nearest wall and licked across my lips before brushing my tongue with his. I had to break the kiss to breathe, and instantly regretted it, searching out his mouth once more. "It'll never be enough, no matter how many times we kiss, it won't be enough," I murmured against his kiss-swollen lips. He braced his hands against the wall on both sides of my head and ground his hardness against my own, eliciting a groan from me at the delicious friction. "Get in our bed, now."

At my desperate and whispered command, James froze for a second and met my heated gaze. "Our bed, I like the sound of that," he said.

"Oh, I love the sound of that. But I'll love it even more when I'm inside you, and you're under me begging for more." I pinned him with what I hoped was a smoldering look, and a raised brow. He returned my look with eyes so full of lust, if we didn't make it to our bed soon, we'd both burn up from the raw heat always simmering between us that was now an inferno.

"Get in here," he urged, and pulled me into the room before flinging me onto the bed. I bounced around for a second before he was crawling on top of me and kissing me once again. Somehow, we managed to get our clothes off, and the frenzy to be together as one ignited to an even more intense level than it had been a moment before.

As I slid into him, there was only one thought on my mind—*finally.*

THE END

About The Author

BL Maxwell grew up in a small town listening to her grandfather spin tales about his childhood. Later she became an avid reader and after a certain vampire series she became obsessed with fanfiction. She soon discovered Slash fanfiction and later discovered the MM genre and was hooked. Many years later, she decided to take the plunge and write down some of the stories that seem to run through her head late at night when she's trying to sleep.

Contact:

Email: blmaxwell.writer@gmail.com

https://smart.bio/blmaxwellwriter/

Also by BL Maxwell

Thank you for reading Ghost Hexed. All books in this series are based on real hauntings in or around Sacramento California.

VALLEY GHOSTS series

Green Eyed Boy, Lobster Tales Book One, is available Here:

https://mybook.to/GreenEyedBoy

Two strangers, drawn together over their work ethic, and sealing the deal over delicious lobster rolls. They could just be the perfect match.

After quitting his job, Billie Watts hits all the food festivals he can as he drives across the country. When he finally reaches Stoney Brook, Maine, he's excited to find he's there just in time to try one of the lobster rolls he's heard so much about. The bright neon yellow food truck with a giant red lobster on top looks like the perfect place to try it.

Lance Karl is as ready as he can be for the start of the three-day Tall Ships Festival and hopes to sell enough lobster rolls out of his food truck to make a good start towards owning a restaurant. The day begins cold and misty, and a text from his nephew saying he can't help him is not the perfect start he'd hoped for.

When a green-eyed stranger interrupts his frantic morning, Lance doesn't realize meeting Billie will not only change his day, but maybe even the rest of his life. Two strangers, drawn together over their work ethic, and sealing the deal over delicious lobster rolls. They could just be the perfect match. A small-town MM Vacation romance.#friends to lovers #meetcute #workplace romance #mm romance

Brown Eyed Boy, Lobster Tales Book Two, New Release

https://mybook.to/BrownEyedBoy

Lance and Billie met and fell in love over their mutual love of food and their drive to have a successful business in the small town of Stoney

Brook Maine. Both are driven to succeed, but now it's time for a vacation, a real vacation.

Billie plans a trip to Dublin, Ireland to explore Lance's Irish roots, he takes a little convincing. But when Billie tells him they'll be spending time with an uncle who also runs a small café, it's more than Lance can resist.

They spend their days trying new foods, exploring ancient wonders, and meeting more new relatives than either of them could have imagined. And at an ancient castle, Lance discovers that everything he needs is right in front of him.

What starts as a vacation ends up being life changing, and something Lance and Billie will never forget.

#VacationRomance #WorkplaceRomance #MMRomance #GayRomance #FriendsToLovers

Enjoy a Free copy of Try To Remember. A short story with Andy and Link.

https://blmaxwellwriter.com/free-reads/

And a Free copy of A Night To Remember. A short story with Sam and Erik.

https://books2read.com/u/baDrw8

Preorder The Things We Lose: https://my-book.to/TTWLose

Preorder Faded Dreams: https://www.amazon.com/Faded-Dreams-BL-Maxwell-ebook/dp/B0CCCN7SC4

BETTER TO-GETHER series

Better Together

Chains Required

The First Twelve

The Better Together Boxset

THE STONE series

Stone Under Skin

Blood Beneath Stone

Stone Hearts

The Stone Series Box Set

SMALL TOWN CITY series

Remember When

A Night to Remember (Short Story)

Try To Forget

Try To Remember (Short Story)

One Last Chance

CONSORTIUM TRILOGY

Burning Addiction

Freezing Aversion

FOUR PACKS Trilogy

The Slow Death

The Ultimate Sacrifice

The Final Salvation

STANDALONE

The List

Double Black Diamonds

Ride: The Chance of a Lifetime

Check Yes or No

A Ghost of a Chance

Tutu

Salt & Lime

Amos Ridge

Six Months

Ten or Fifteen Miles

The Snake in the Castle

Green Eyed Boy

A Beach Far Away

The Things We Find

Blinding Light

Peppermint Mocha Kisses

Small Town City Series

Remember When

BL Maxwell

https://mybook.to/RememberWhenA

A night to remember, a confession, and a lifetime of love in this small town, friends to lovers Christmas romance.

Andrew Lawson's life in Sacramento has turned from being everything he dreamed of growing up, to a lonely place where finding someone special to share his life with is impossible. When the first person he meets on returning home for Thanksgiving is his childhood friend Link, it's a reminder of happier times when his whole future lay in front of him. Agreeing to a drink before heading to his parent's place is a way to reconnect, and a great way to start the holiday.

Link Stanton never considered leaving the small farming town he grew up in, but he misses Andy more than he'll ever admit. Secretly lusting after a friend is bad enough but being in love with him is so much worse. One drink with friends seems harmless enough, after all, catching up on old times can't be a bad thing, until beers turn to shots, and Link reveals how he really feels.

Everything could change, and if Andrew doesn't remember Link's heartfelt confession, they could carry on as friends. But, if he does remember, this could be either the worst, or the best, Christmas of all. #smalltownromance #Holidayromance #mmromance #Christmas #friendstolovers

Try To Forget

BL Maxwell

https://mybook.to/TryToForget

After being dumped by his boyfriend, spending the weekend alone wasn't something Sam Braun was looking forward to. So, when the hairstylist that works next to his bookstore invites him to his hometown for the weekend, Sam jumps at the chance. Visiting the small town of Occident could be just what he needs to forget, at least for a few days.

Erik Thorne has lived his whole life in the same town where nothing new ever happens, and any stranger who comes to town is always a big deal. When his old friend Andy brings a friend home for the weekend, Erik is drawn to the man in a way that confuses him at first. But his curiosity about the gorgeous blond from the city gets the better of him, and he can't resist spending more time with him.

Sam was hoping to forget his troubles when he meets Erik. While Erik can't seem to think of anything besides the city boy with the bookstore he can't wait to visit. Distance might not be the only thing that stands between them, as they find out admitting what you want isn't always easy. Each book can be read as a standalone. #AgeGap, #MMRomance, #FriendsToLovers #OppositesAttract #SmallTownRomance #City/Country

One Last Chance (New Release)

https://mybook.to/OLCSmalltown

Stu Lawson had always lived in the small town of Occident. He'd been born a farmer, and he was more than happy to stay a farmer even when his dad decided it wasn't the life for him. He's been raising his daughter since the day she was born, and he's never regretted being a single dad, but Stu has a few secrets.

Morgan Grant was born into a life he never wanted and had done everything he could to avoid. Staying drunk helps him forget and numbs the pain he can't bring himself to face. After a long night of drinking, he ends up dumped in a small town north of Sacramento without money, his phone, or a way to get back to the city he calls home.

Stu's focus has always been his daughter, but he can't control his curiosity about the stranger who shows up in Occident alone in the middle of the night. He offers to help, even when he knows he shouldn't. Old feelings rise to the surface and he's helpless to ignore them, or Morgan. This stranger could be his chance at happiness, or his downfall. #singledad #gayromance #stranded #smalltownromance #secrets

Peppermint Mocha Kisses

https://mybook.to/PeppermintMK

Randy Miller wants nothing more than to make a living selling the fantastic cookies he dreams up when he's not working as a web designer. He's always loved baking, but he's afraid of taking the leap from hobby to business. Mostly he's afraid of failing, and of Eli coming up with a better recipe.

Eli Canton has a crush. A big crush on someone who avoids him whenever he can. Eli loves everything about Randy, even if he's grouchy and seems to work way too much. Eli knows he's not all bad and hopes to have a chance with him someday.

A broken oven throws the two of them together, and even though Randy doesn't want to admit it, he likes the time he spends with Eli. And Eli definitely can't wait to spend more time with Randy. Now if only they can make it past the annual cookie exchange and possibly Valentine's Day to their own sweet happy ending. #smalltown Romance, #opposites attract, #MM Romance

The Ultimate Sacrifice (Four Packs Trilogy Book 2)

https://mybook.to/FourPacksTrilogy

Grady Summerville is facing a slow and agonizing death, but has come to terms with his disease and doesn't fear dying. However, fate has other ideas, presenting him with a future thanks to Max Steele. Grady owes his very life to Max, and as his health improves, finds himself falling head over heels with his savior.

Max Steele has been forced to leave his pack and everyone he knows to move to the West Territory to be a blood donor for Grady. He knows it's the right thing to do, but it doesn't mean he has to like it.

As tensions escalate between the two packs, Max finds his loyalty tested and is torn between following his alpha, or following his heart.

If Max doesn't make the sacrifice then it will be Grady making the ultimate sacrifice and paying with his life. #MMParanormal #Shifters

Freezing Aversion (Consortium Trilogy Book Two)

The cold isn't the only killer in the wilderness.
https://mybook.to/FreezingAversion

Benjamin Coulton is a tracker employed by the Consortium, the ruling counsel of vampires. When he's sent to investigate a rogue vampire killing indiscriminately in a remote region of Alaska. Bad weather hampers his effort and he loses the vampire he's been tasked to find.

Leon Davis and his friend Trevor agreed to be winter caretakers for several cabins and a fishing lodge, thinking it would be easy money. They settle into their daily routine of checking the cabins for animal break-ins, or broken water pipes, and prepare for a long winter.

Until a run in with a vampire changes everything.

Ben finds a newly turned vampire left for dead by the rogue vampire, and suddenly Ben's mission changes course. In the freezing wilderness of Alaska, he uncovers more truths and the mate he'd always longed for... and now the vampire he was tasked to find is hunting them. #MMParanormalRomance #vampire #fatedmate #thriller

A Ghost of a Chance

https://mybook.to/AGhostOfAChance

James McKinney has always lived life alone. He doesn't have a family, at least none that he remembers. He's always dreamed of having a house of his own, a place he can call home. Finding the right house, ready to work to make it his home, nothing can put a damper on his happiness, or can it? Trey Andral, returning home from college, notices someone moving into his old friend's house next door. Miss Hattie is still waving to him from the bedroom window, even though he knows she's gone. He also knows he can't not help the new guy make the house his own. Trey has always been able to see and hear sprits, but what's normal to him is terrifying to most others. When the spirits seem intent on contacting James, Trey has no choice but to share his secret, risking their friendship. If they work together, maybe they can figure out what the clues the spirits are giving them mean. And maybe they can find family in each other.

Tutu (Malicious Gods: Egypt)

https://mybook.to/Tutu

Kit Nelson was thrown into the world of demons and cults as a child. He's learned to depend on no one, and to do all he can to keep himself safe from dark forces. He also knows he can't trust anyone else with his life. He knows what the demons who hunt him have in mind for him, and he'll fight it every step of the way.

Tommy Smythe and his sister Lola have been fighting what they know is a rising tide of evil for years. They're prepared with all their paranormal weaponry, including the assistance of an ancient god who has fought demons his whole existence. Tutu, the Egyptian god and Master of Demons has chosen Tommy to be his vessel and his sword when needed to destroy any and all demons.

A new threat ripples through the dark underworld, one that will be felt across all mankind. A demon has chosen one whose body he will use to return to the land of the living. But only if Kit, Tommy, and Lola can't stop him. Only Tutu has the power and knowledge to protect them from the demon Rerek, and he also knows even with his help, this is not going to be an easy battle.

Amos Ridge

https://mybook.to/AmosRidge

"There's no time. Remember, I love you."It all started with a discovery. A cave beneath a waterfall that held a crystal. Two boys—best friends—embark on a journey they're told will help all mankind. As the years go by, their friendship turns to love, and their adventure turns into a battle.Drew Langly is the keeper of the crystal. With his contact, the crystal allows them to jump to different timestreams and help, if they can, to further that society or fix anything that improves their lives. When he's ripped from the timestream, it's the beginning of what will change everything they've come to know about how the different timestreams function.Colby Adams is Drew's boyfriend, fellow traveler, and jump partner. When Drew is left vulnerable after a failed jump, he's there to help and try to figure out what went wrong. They soon discover another team of travelers is in trouble, but they've been warned against trusting them. The more they learn, the more they realize everything has been a lie. To rewrite a history that's been full of deceit, they'll need to put their trust, once again, in strangers. Can they rewind it all and begin again? Experience the history they were always meant to? With some unconventional help, maybe...

Milton Keynes UK
Ingram Content Group UK Ltd.
UKHW010659210823
427162UK00004B/110